UnderWorld
Ambush

adapted by Jake Black

Grosset & Dunlap
An Imprint of Penguin Group (USA) Inc.

GROSSET & DUNLAP
Published by the Penguin Group
Penguin Group (USA) Inc., 375 Hudson Street, New York, New York 10014, USA
Penguin Group (Canada), 90 Eglinton Avenue East, Suite 700,
Toronto, Ontario M4P 2Y3, Canada (a division of Pearson Penguin Canada Inc.)
Penguin Books Ltd., 80 Strand, London WC2R 0RL, England
Penguin Group Ireland, 25 St. Stephen's Green, Dublin 2, Ireland
(a division of Penguin Books Ltd.)
Penguin Group (Australia), 250 Camberwell Road, Camberwell, Victoria 3124, Australia
(a division of Pearson Australia Group Pty. Ltd.)
Penguin Books India Pvt. Ltd., 11 Community Centre,
Panchsheel Park, New Delhi—110 017, India
Penguin Group (NZ), 67 Apollo Drive, Rosedale, North Shore 0632, New Zealand
(a division of Pearson New Zealand Ltd.)
Penguin Books (South Africa) (Pty.) Ltd., 24 Sturdee Avenue,
Rosebank, Johannesburg 2196, South Africa

Penguin Books Ltd., Registered Offices:
80 Strand, London WC2R 0RL, England

Library of Congress Control Number: 2009032521

ISBN 978-0-448-45398-9   10 9 8 7 6 5 4 3 2 1

Welcome to Perim, a strange land divided into four Tribes— OverWorld, UnderWorld, Mipedian, and Danian.

These Tribes of Creatures have been at war with each other for centuries. Their epic battles were the basis for Chaotic, a popular game among humans. Each Tribe is full of Creatures who use unique Attacks and Battlegear in their struggle to dominate Perim. Despite years of conflict, the four Tribes faced a threat from the outside that was bigger than they'd ever known. The M'arrillians, a Tribe from Perim believed to only be a myth, were invading. The M'arrillians used Attacks that were different from the other Tribes. These Attacks were liquid-based, and could do a great deal of damage. But even more dangerous was the M'arrillians' ability to take control of another Creature's mind, and bend his will to theirs! The M'arrillians, led by the mysterious Aa'une, set out to take over all of Perim.

Between Earth and Perim is Chaotic, where humans would play the game of the same name. While players could compete against one another on Earth by playing the card game, in Chaotic, they become their favorite Creatures in Drome matches.

Chapter 1

The M'arrillian invasion was making it difficult for Chaotic players to 'port to Perim to get scans of Creatures, Locations, Attacks, and Battlegear. These scans became harder to get as the

M'arrillians advanced throughout the land. Many human players were sad to learn that the minds of many of the Creatures of Perim had been taken over by the M'arrillians.

One of these human players, Kaz Kalinkas, was determined to free his friend H'earring from the M'arrillians' control. It would be dangerous, but Kaz didn't care. He just wanted to rescue his friend.

The M'arrillians were building a canal that would allow them to flood the Marsh of Murk, a key Location in the UnderWorld. The M'arrillians were known for flooding parts of Perim; it gave them a tactical advantage in battling the Tribes. H'earring was one of several Creatures the M'arrillians had taken over and were forcing to build the canal. From behind several rocks,

Kaz watched and planned his move. When the moment was right, he would leap into action, and rescue H'earring. Suddenly, two M'arrillian guards appeared behind him. Kaz tried to run, but he wasn't fast enough. The M'arrillians blasted Energy bolts at Kaz, knocking him to the ground.

Chapter 2

On this particular day, Kaz's friends Tom, Sarah, and Peyton were watching a Chaotic match in the PortCourt, a gathering place for Chaotic players. There they shared food and fun times with their fellow Chaotic friends.

Today's match featured a M'arrillian named Rath'tab against a Danian called Khavakk, and it wasn't going well for the Danian player. Rath'tab was winning.

"Ever since the M'arrillians showed up, Drome matches have gotten uglier and uglier," Sarah said.

"It's not just Drome matches. It's all of Perim. That river where they're fighting is all blech!" Peyton agreed.

Rath'tab blasted Khavakk with an attack to take over his mind.

"These M'arrillians are a pain in the brain!" Peyton said.

Suddenly, a strange, golden headband appeared on Khavakk's head. The headband freed Khavakk from the M'arrillian's control and allowed the Danian to blast an attack of his own.

"That headband gives you a mental block!" Peyton said excitedly. All this talk of M'arrillians and Perim made Tom think of his best friend Kaz

and his mission to rescue H'earring from the M'arrillians. Tom decided to contact Kaz using his scanner. Kaz's face appeared on the small screen. His eyes were wide and emotionless. Tom knew something was wrong.

"Kaz, are you okay?" Tom asked.

"This human now belongs to the M'arrillians," Kaz said slowly.

"You're controlling Kaz?" Tom gasped in shock.

"Yes," Kaz replied, his mind clearly under M'arrillian control. "And anyone who interferes with our plans will meet the same fate. You have been warned."

The scanner went dark as Tom rejoined his

friends at their table. Things in the Drome match were getting worse. Rath'tab was blasting a series of attacks at Khavakk.

"Guys, they got Kaz," Tom said grimly.

Sarah and Peyton turned to face Tom in shock.

"Kaz. He went to save H'earring, and the M'arrillians took control of his mind. We've got to save him!" Tom said, growing a little panicked.

"Of course we'll save him," Peyton said.

"We'll find that MindBander headband Khavakk used in the match," Sarah said.

Tom nodded, knowing the MindBander would free Kaz's mind, and raced away. "I'm heading to the Marsh of Murk to find Kaz. You find the MindBander!"

Chapter 3

Deep in Perim's UnderWorld, the Tribe's leader, Chaor, gathered together his army. They examined a map of the UnderWorld, marking the path the M'arrillians had taken.

Chaor was angry that his enemies had flooded the Lava Pond, but was pleased that they were building the canal toward the Marsh of Murk. He knew he and his army could stop the enemy Creatures and protect the UnderWorld.

Chaor planned to have his military commander, Takinom, lead a team into the middle of the Marsh of Murk. The marsh, he

knew, was an oil field. Takinom and her crew would use their powerful Fire Attacks to ignite the oil field into a raging fire to stop the M'arrillians. Chaor and his band of soldiers would arrive with his giant Annihilizer and finish the job.

"But, Chaor, is that really necessary?" Agitos, one of Chaor's advisors, asked.

Chaor glared at him. "They have taken over our homes, and have shown us no mercy! They will receive none!"

Chaor's army marched out toward the battlefield near the Marsh of Murk. From high atop his massive Viledriver, Chaor addressed his loyal followers.

"Today we make UnderWorld history because these M'arrillians will *be* history!" Chaor laughed. A cheer went up from the UnderWorld army.

"All right, let's move out!" Chaor ordered. His forces gathered behind him and the massive army trudged toward the oily marsh. In the air above, Takinom and her soldiers soared in front of the army traveling on the ground. The assault on the M'arrillians would be fast.

Meanwhile, across the UnderWorld, the mysterious M'arrillian leader, Aa'une, used his powerful telepathy to communicate with Phelphor, a Fluidmorpher Scout for the M'arrillians.

"Phelphor," Aa'une's mind called out, "what is the status of our canal at the Marsh of Murk?"

"It is all going to plan. And the UnderWorlders are coming, just as you predicted," Phelphor communicated back to his master.

Aa'une smiled and closed the communication by saying, "It is time."

Phelphor closed his mind from the telepathic communication and said, "You are a M'arrillian now." Phelphor turned to face the brainwashed Lord Van Bloot, an UnderWorlder. "You will stop

Chaor and his army. Don't fail us!"

Lord Van Bloot took his place at the head of his army—a group of other UnderWorlders whose minds had also been taken over by the M'arrillians.

"We will not fail," Lord Van Bloot promised. He soared above his army, about to betray the UnderWorld!

Chapter 4

Chaor's troops closed in on the M'arrillian's canal. Chaor looked over the region and ordered Takinom and her soldiers to take flight and attack.

"Time for Operation Obliteration," Chaor said menacingly.

Takinom and a group of UnderWorlders flew toward the canal. Takinom blasted a small bolt of Energy at a pair of M'arrillian guards floating above the canal a short distance from Kaz and the other diggers. The blast bounced off one of the M'arrillians causing it to notice Takinom and her fellow soldiers.

"That should attract some attention," Takinom said proudly.

The injured M'arrillian floated away out of Takinom's sight.

On the far side of the canal, Tom appeared. He'd used his scanner to 'port from the PortCourt in Chaotic to the Marsh of Murk in Perim.

"Gross," Tom said as he stepped in the oily marsh. But he didn't have much time to get used to his surroundings. Two large M'arrillians

approached. Tom took a step backward, scared.
Just as the M'arrillians were about to attack, they
were alerted to the UnderWorlders' invasion.
Tom was saved as the M'arrillian soldiers turned
back to fight Chaor's forces. The battle between
the UnderWorlders and the M'arrillians was about
to begin.

Chapter 5

On a ridge high above the Marsh of Murk,
Chaor called for his army to prepare the
Annihilizer, a gigantic Battlegear that could
completely destroy the M'arrillians. The vast

UnderWorld army scrambled to carry out their ruler's orders.

Takinom and her small band of flying UnderWorlders landed on the ground near the M'arrillian forces. The two sides exchanged blows, blasting intense bolts of Energy back and forth at each other. A M'arrillian shot a glowing sphere at Takinom. The winged, warrior woman

flew in the air, avoiding the Energy. She used her own Battlegear to turn another M'arrillian flare back on the M'arrillian. The battle was growing in intensity with each passing second!

Tom hid behind the rocks that surrounded the canal. He was trying to stay out of the way, but he was also desperately trying to find Kaz. Scurrying behind the rocks, Tom avoid being hit by the flying explosions around him. He peeked out from behind a rock and saw Kaz below working mindlessly in the canal trench.

Tom knew this was his chance. He slid down the rock face toward his friend in the trench.

"Kaz! Kaz!" Tom called out. But it was no use. Tom ran past a pair of UnderWorlders who had been enslaved by the M'arrillians. They didn't notice the human running through the trench, trying to rescue Kaz.

"Kaz, the M'arrillians are controlling your mind," Tom pleaded. "Get your scanner and 'port back to Chaotic and you'll be okay."

Again, Kaz ignored him. Tom was frustrated. He didn't know what else he could do to save his friend. Without warning, Kaz turned to face Tom. He thought Kaz had finally heard him calling out to him and was going to return to Chaotic. But he was wrong. Kaz, H'earring, and the

other Creatures that the M'arrillians were controlling raced to help in the battle against the UnderWorlders. Kaz was in greater danger than before. Tom grabbed him by the arm.

"Kaz, stop!" he yelled.

Kaz shoved Tom to the ground, breaking free of his best friend's grip. Tom glared back at Kaz.

"We can do this the easy way or the hard way,"

Tom warned as he jumped to grab Kaz. His leap was unsuccessful, however, as H'earring blasted Tom with a burst of sand and dirt, knocking him back to the ground. H'earring and Kaz ran back toward the battlefront. Tom was desperate to save Kaz but he had no idea how.

Chapter 6

Deep in an underground Danian incubation chamber, Sarah and Peyton searched for the powerful headband that could free Kaz's mind from the M'arrillians. They had talked to the Chaotic player, Danian Dan, who had used the headband in his match earlier. Danian Dan said he'd hidden the headband in one of the eggshells in the murky chamber.

Peyton and Sarah rifled through egg after egg searching for the headband until Sarah's scanner beeped. It was Tom calling to find out what was taking so long.

"There are hundreds of eggs down here," she said.

"Hurry, Sarah," Tom pleaded. "I don't know how much time Kaz has left!"

Peyton looked inside an egg. A baby Danian popped up from the broken shell.

"Aw, isn't it cute!" Peyton said. The baby

Danian responded by biting Peyton's nose.

"We're looking as fast as we can, Tommy!"
Peyton yelled out as he rubbed his sore nose.

Tom was more anxious. "Kaz and I may not last
much longer out here!"

Sarah and Peyton continued their search. With
so many eggs, it seemed hopeless. Then Sarah
called out to Peyton. "Found it!"

"Well, let's get out of here!" Peyton shouted back.

In a colorful display of light, Peyton and
Sarah transported out of the Danian incubation
chamber and near the Marsh of Murk. Things
were obviously dangerous in the battle. The two
humans could see smoke rising from the canal
the M'arrillians were trying to build.

Sarah pulled out her scanner and called Tom.
"Where are you?" Sarah asked.

Tom was in the middle of the canal, chasing after Kaz. "I'm here in the marsh, trying to get Kaz out."

"We're by the marsh. We have the MindBander!" Peyton yelled into the scanner over the battle noise.

Tom looked up from the trench and could see his friends.

"Wait for me," he said into his scanner. "I'll be right there."

Chapter 7

Overlooking the battleground, Chaor and his troops prepared the Annihilizer. It whirred and roared as it powered up. A group of UnderWorld soldiers used the levers and switches to get the massive cannon ready to fire. Chaor watched the battle below and was not pleased. Several of Takinom's aerial warriors had fallen under M'arrillian control. A few had even dropped their Torweggs—Battlegear that allowed them to fly. The fierce fight seemed to be going in the M'arrillians' favor, and Chaor was not happy.

"The Annihilizer is almost ready, Chaor," one

of the UnderWorld guards said.

Chaor marched his way to the main firing switch on the Annihilizer, determined to destroy his foes once and for all.

"Time to get rid of some M'arrillians," Chaor said as he curled his fingers around the firing lever.

Chaor pulled the lever. A massive fireball formed in the barrel of the cannonlike Annihilizer and shot toward the trench.

Takinom looked up and saw the fire that was about to rain down on the canal and her troops. "Get moving," she called out.

The UnderWorld soldiers withdrew quickly, not wanting to be in the path of the fireball when it reached the oily field and ignited the trench in a massive flame.

Takinom was followed closely by Rarran. Several M'arrillians tried to escape the trench as well, but with no luck. One M'arrillian hit Rarran with a small bolt of Energy, but it seemed to have no effect. Kaz wandered aimlessly around, unsure where to go or what to do. As the fireball grew closer, it looked like certain doom for Kaz, and the M'arrillians.

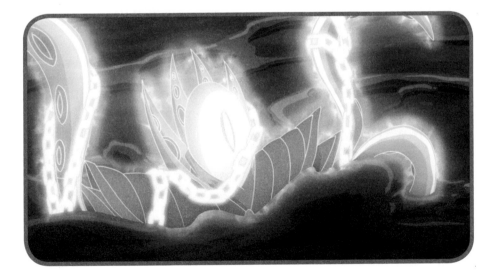

Suddenly, from behind, Tom swooped in from the sky and grabbed Kaz. He was wearing a Torwegg. Tom and Kaz flew out of the battleground toward the ridge where Sarah and Peyton waited. If they could get there without being hit by the Attacks from the M'arrillians or UnderWorlders, Tom could finally save his friend.

Just as Tom and Kaz soared skyward, the

massive fireball of the Annihilizer exploded in the middle of the Marsh of Murk. A gigantic explosion rose out of the ground, lighting up the whole area. Fire consumed everything. On the ridge near the Marsh, Peyton and Sarah shielded their eyes trying to figure out if their friends had survived the blast. But Tom and Kaz were nowhere to be seen!

Chapter 8

Tom and Kaz landed safely a short distance from the fiery explosion in the canal. Sarah and Peyton raced to greet them. Peyton put the MindBander headband on Kaz's head. The MindBander glimmered in the light, and suddenly Kaz's mind was free from the M'arrillians' control.

"Welcome back, Kazzer," Peyton said as Kaz removed the headband, coming back to normal.

"H'earring? Where's H'earring?" Kaz said, a little panicked as he observed the explosive chaos around the canal.

Sarah, Tom, and Peyton shook their heads sadly. It seemed H'earring was lost forever in the explosion. Sarah put her hand on Kaz's shoulder to try to comfort him.

"At least Chaor beat the M'arrillians," she said.

"Guys, look!" Tom said happily, staring at his scanner. Using his scanner like a telescope, Tom could see H'earring and several other Creatures crawling out of the fiery swampland.

"H'earring made it!" Kaz yelled out excitedly.

The other kids cheered, happy that Kaz's friend survived.

Takinom and Rarran landed in front of Chaor and revealed that Rarran had used a Fire Repellant Attack on H'earring and the others just before the fireball hit. That was how they survived.

"Good job, Rarran," Chaor said.

Rarran looked at Chaor, his eyes wide. "I am no longer Rarran," he said. "I am Aa'une, supreme leader of the M'arrillians, and you are Chaor, former ruler of the UnderWorld."

Chaor and his solders looked on in shock.

"What's that supposed to mean?" Chaor demanded. Rarran, under Aa'une's control, smiled. "This was a trap. We lured you away from UnderWorld City. There, Lord Van Bloot

and his army took over the city. It is now under M'arrillian control. Your Tribe has turned against you, and is now under the M'arrillians' control!"

Chaor growled. There was nothing he could do. He had fallen for the M'arrillians' trap. The M'arrillians he thought he'd defeated with the fireball had actually hidden in the oil until the flames died down. The UnderWorld had been overthrown.

Chaor, Takinom, and their army pulled back to regroup. The M'arrillian takeover of Perim was only beginning, but Chaor knew that even though the UnderWorld lost this battle, they would eventually win the war.